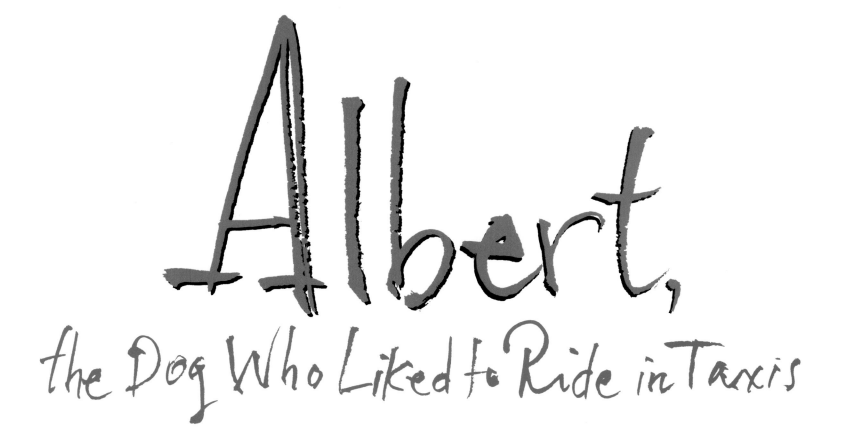

Albert,
the Dog Who Liked to Ride in Taxis

story by CYNTHIA ZARIN   illustrations by PIERRE PRATT

A RICHARD JACKSON BOOK • ATHENEUM BOOKS FOR YOUNG READERS

NEW YORK   LONDON   TORONTO   SYDNEY   SINGAPORE

Atheneum Books for Young Readers
An imprint of Simon & Schuster
Children's Publishing Division
1230 Avenue of the Americas
New York, New York 10020
Text copyright © 2004 by Cynthia Zarin
Illustrations copyright © 2004 by Pierre Pratt

Book design by Abelardo Martínez
The text of this book is set in Mrs Eaves.
The illustrations are rendered in acrylic.

Manufactured in China
First Edition
10 9 8 7 6 5 4 3 2 1
Library of Congress Cataloging-in-Publication Data
Zarin, Cynthia.
Albert, the dog who liked to ride in taxis / Cynthia Zarin ;
illustrated by Pierre Pratt.—1st ed.
p.   cm.
"A Richard Jackson Book."
Summary: Albert the dachshund loves nothing better than riding in taxicabs,
until the day a taxicab adventure takes him to the airport.
ISBN 0-689-84762-9
[1. Dachshunds—Fiction. 2. Dogs—Fiction. 3. Taxicabs—Fiction. 4. New York
(New York)—Fiction.] I. Pratt, Pierre, ill. II. Title.
PZ7 .Z263 Al 2004
[E]—dc21   2002005293

For Rose, who saw Albert first
—C. Z.

To taxi drivers everywhere
—P. P.

Albert liked to ride in taxis. Every morning he woke up filled with hope and sniffed the air for rain. If it rained, Albert knew, Mrs. Crabtree might take a taxi.

Nothing was worse for him than to hear the doorman say, "Nice day, Albert," when he left the building in the morning.

On nice days Mrs. Crabtree walked. Winter, spring, and fall, Albert and Mrs. Crabtree walked the children, Sam and Rebecca Crabtree, to school. They walked to the market. They walked to pick up Mr. Crabtree's shirts at the dry cleaner, and they walked in the park. When it rained they took taxis.

Once in a very great while, Mrs. Crabtree took a taxi unexpectedly. It was usually around Christmas, when she was laden with packages. "Oh, Albert," she said at such times, "I am sorry but I don't think I can manage."

To Albert her words were the best Christmas presents of all. Sitting upright on a gaily wrapped package next to Mrs. Crabtree in the taxi, he could spot some of his friends as he rode through the park. He could see Hortense, a poodle who was nice enough, but inclined to be huffy, and Malcolm, the retriever who lived around the corner. Riding past them Albert felt like a prince. He tilted his head, slightly.

These holiday excursions were Albert's best times, better even than his taxi rides on rainy days when he often had to endure indignities. "Make sure that dog doesn't wet the seat, lady," the driver might snarl at Mrs. Crabtree. Or worse, "NO DOGS!" More than once Albert gazed sadly at the back of a taxi as it roared away.

Of course, Albert had other pleasures. He liked to greet the Crabtree children on the steps of their school, and pretend to knock over their friends. He liked to roll in leaves. He liked musicals, and he was happy when Mr. Crabtree, who liked them too, played *Oklahoma!* after dinner.

But most of all Albert liked to ride in taxis.

Life went on in an ordinary way for some time, until one day something unexpected happened.

Mrs. Crabtree and Albert were standing together chatting with Tony the doorman, having dropped some letters into the mailbox on the corner. Albert was off his leash, a happy circumstance that occurred if Mrs. Crabtree was not planning to go far.

It was a quiet day. The children were at school.

Mr. Crabtree had flown off on a business trip.

From behind Tony's trouser leg Albert watched as a taxi, like a huge yellow fish, swam up and stopped in front of the building. The strong foot of Mrs. Milton, who lived on the fifth floor, stepped out.

Albert watched the foot as if in a trance. He couldn't help himself. When the rest of Mrs. Milton got out of the taxi, Albert, quickly, quietly, and with a pounding heart, jumped in.

No one noticed.

Mrs. Crabtree went on talking to Tony.

Mrs. Milton slammed the taxi's door shut, and with Albert crouched down in the backseat, the taxi pulled away.

Albert had never been so excited in his life. Here was luxury. Here was freedom. Cautiously he raised his head up on his front paws and craftily sneaked a look out the window. The air was sweet. The green park was approaching. There, coming out of the gate, was his friend Hortense. Forgetting himself entirely, Albert barked.

The driver slammed on the brakes, leapt out of the taxi, scooped up Albert, and dumped him onto the sidewalk. "NO DOGS!"

Albert was disconsolate. How could he have been so stupid? But then an idea occurred to him. If he could jump into one taxi, why not another?

Out of the corner of his eye he saw Hortense nearing his building. He would tell her the wonderful news. Perhaps she would accompany him!

"Hortense, Hortense!" called Albert.

When they reached the building Hortense looked down her nose at Albert. "I don't speak to stray dogs," she said, and stepped into the revolving door.

Can it be, Albert thought, *she doesn't recognize me? Am I nothing without my leash? Without Mrs. Crabtree?* He plunged into the revolving door.

On the first go-round he caught a glimpse of Hortense heading to the elevator, but when he tried to follow her, he found his way was blocked. Around and around went the door with Albert trapped inside. How was he going to get out? Just as he was plunging into despair, a very old lady stepped in beside him.

The old lady pushed only lightly on the door. It slowed down, and Albert was able to slip out. A taxi pulled up to the curb, and when the old lady stepped into it, Albert, NATURALLY, hopped in after her.

"Eighty-eighth and Fifth," the old lady said to the driver.

Then she looked down and saw Albert.

"Hello," she said. The old lady had a high and quavery voice. "Are you mine?" she asked. "I once had a dog who looked very much like you. Her name was Alexandra."

Albert opened his mouth to answer—for he had had a great-aunt named Alexandra—but the old lady put an admonishing finger to her lips.

"*Shh!*" she said, pointing to the back of the driver's neck. "He'll *hear* you." She mouthed words so that no sound came out.

"What's your name?" the old lady asked.

Albert told her.

"Ah." The old lady sighed. "Albert. That was the name of my late husband. How I have missed having a companion!"

From her large handbag the old lady pulled out a big straw hat. She put it on. "Albert," she said, "tomorrow I am going on a trip to the Kalahari Desert. Would you like to accompany me? It would be a great adventure for us both."

Albert looked back at the old lady. A great adventure indeed! Anything, he saw now, could happen in a taxi!

The taxi pulled up to the curb.

At that moment, through the window, he spotted his friend Malcolm.

He was not alone. Today he was accompanied by Max the corgi; Duchess, a German shepherd; Mouse, a sheepdog; and Colette, a schnauzer from Ninety-first Street. Their leashes were held—loosely, yes, but held nonetheless—by a bespectacled young man who trotted after them.

"Hey, Malcolm!" shouted Albert, forgetting the old lady, the Kalahari, and even the taxi. The taxi window was open, and Albert jumped out.

"Malcolm, my old pal," cried Albert, catching up. "So good to see you. You can wish me *bon voyage.* I am off on a journey with my friend, who is just now packing her bags for the Kalahari."

"Better bring your water dish." Max smirked. "Dry as a bone out there."

Jealous, that's what they are, Albert thought. He stuck his nose in the air. A hand circled his neck.

"I *thought* it was you," said the bespectacled young man. "Albert, Mrs. Crabtree must be crazy with worry!"

"Rruff!" With all his strength Albert resisted. He jerked away from the young man and dived into the tangle of leashes he held in his hand.

"Bark, woof, aargh!" Colette ran one way. Malcolm another. The young man tried to run after Max, who was off his leash and crazy with happiness.

"Take me with you, Albert!" Max shouted as Albert neatly crossed Ninetieth Street, where, like a beacon of light, a yellow door stood open.

A taxi. Escape! Shelter! Behind him the door slammed shut. Max, hard on his heels, yapped at the window.

"Have you lost a friend?" a high voice inquired.

Albert looked up. The voice belonged to a boy wearing blue jeans and a gray sweatshirt. An older boy was sitting beside him.

"We're going to California to visit our grandmother," the younger boy continued.

Albert explained that he had been heading to the Kalahari, but California sounded equally interesting.

"He's not our dog," said the older boy sternly. "We can't just take him."

"Don't be so stuffy, Horace," said the younger boy.

Albert, sensing a crisis, offered the boy his paw.

"See, he *wants* to come. Please? My name is Wallace," he said to Albert as an afterthought.

Albert looked out the window. They were beyond the park and driving over a big bridge. The light was soft and dusk was coming on. The city glimmered, and Albert felt his old life—the Crabtrees, Malcolm, even Tony the doorman—slipping away. He felt sad, but exhilarated. He had ridden in three taxis in one day. He was a dog of the world. He had always known it.

The taxi turned off the highway and began to drive in circles.

"They won't let him on the plane," said Horace.

"He's a *small* dog," said Wallace.

The airport was the busiest place Albert had ever seen. Through a hole in Wallace's backpack, he watched as some people darted this way and that. Others stood in long lines. Doors opened and closed. Whistles blew. Everyone was in a hurry.

But most astonishing of all, through the big plate-glass window, Albert could see airplanes landing and taking off. They looked like big white birds.

How could it be? How could they stay up in the air?

Beside himself with excitement, Albert began to pull at the strap of Wallace's backpack until his head, and then his paws, were sticking out. Could he get closer to the window?

Albert jumped. He hit the polished floor of the airport, running.

"Albert!" shouted Wallace, but his voice was lost in the crowd.

Albert reached the window and rushed madly back and forth, his eyes glued to the sight of the astonishing airplanes. One, he knew, would take Horace and Wallace to California. Another was waiting for the old lady, to fly her to the Kalahari. He stopped for a moment in his running and sighed. He would be happy to go to either of those places.

"Albert!" This time the voice was familiar.

Wallace, Horace, and Mr. Crabtree were standing in a circle around him.

"Is this your dog, sir?" Horace asked Mr. Crabtree.

"Why, yes," said Mr. Crabtree. "Remarkable dog. Seems to have come across town on his own to meet me at the airport."

Wallace, Horace, and Albert looked at one another.

"Bon voyage," said Albert.

"And to you too," said Wallace.

Mr. Crabtree picked Albert up. He strode through the airport doors. "Remarkable," he said, shaking his head, and put up his hand to hail a taxi.

"Ninety-eight Riverside Drive," said Mr. Crabtree. Albert settled down for the ride. It had been a long day. *Taxis are all very well,* he thought to himself, *but can they take you to California? To the Kalahari? To Timbuktu?*

Behind closed eyes Albert started to plan.